THE ENCHANTED FOREST OF ROARING SPRINGS

A Shiny Little Things - Picture Book

Frank M. Stangle

Written and Illustrated by

FRANK STANGLE

8-4-23

2650

The Enchanted Forest of Roaring Springs
Copyright © 2023 Frank Stangle

Produced and printed by Stangle Publications

Visit our website at
www.frankstangle.com
for more information.

First Stangle Publications Edition

ISBN: 9798391087564

Written and illustrated by Frank Stangle

Published by Stangle Publications,
Pohatcong, NJ, USA.

THIS BOOK IS DEDICATED TO ALEXANDRIA, MASON, OLIVIA, AND LENNOX.
YOU HAVE FILLED MY LIFE WITH LOVE,
I NEVER DREAMED I WOULD HAVE KIDS OF MY OWN,
AND THEN ALONG CAME YOU FOUR.
I GET SO EXCITED EVERY TIME I SEE YOU,
AND YOU NEVER FAIL TO SHOWER ME WITH HUGS AND KISSES.
THE WAY YOU RUN INTO MY ARMS OVERFLOWS MY HEART WITH JOY.
YOU ARE THE INSPIRATION THAT HELPS KEEP ME GOING.
I CANT WAIT TO SEE WHAT YOU ALL GROW UP TO BE.
MIMI AND I WILL ALWAYS DO OUR BEST TO MAKE SURE YOU HAVE WHAT YOU NEED.
WE LOVE THE FOUR OF YOU.

POOH-PA

Map of
Roaring Springs

Maiden Creek

Rusty, and Skeeter,

were their names. (2)

One of their favorite places to have fun,
and mess around.

Was in the town of Roaring Springs,
at the playground.

(3)

Next to the playground,
not north, or south, or east, but west.

Sat a mystical and magical place,
The Enchanted Forest.

(4)

But then Alexandria shouted, "Oh my!"
as she saw a horrible sight.

The animals at play,
were now having a fight.

(6)

The dozer trampled the swing set,
and went next for the jungle gym.

When Rusty said, "The animals are still fighting,
there's no way we will stop him."

The kids knew Mr. Louse,
and he was no stranger.

He was just doing his job,
but the animal's home was in danger!
(11)

Alexandria stood at the forest, looked in, and started yelling.

"What is she doing? asked Rusty. Skeeter replied, "There's no way of telling."

The playground was destroyed, the Enchanted Forest was next on the list.

When Skeeter saw something and said, "What a wonderful twist." (12)

Alexandria's little talk,
got the animals on the same team.

They pulled together and stopped Mr. Louse,
or so it may seem.

The dozer stopped and began to smoke,
the whole ordeal was done.

The animals jumped around,
and the kids cheered, "We have won!"

The adults walked away,
with barely a peep.

And the kids went home for dinner,
and some well needed sleep.

(14)

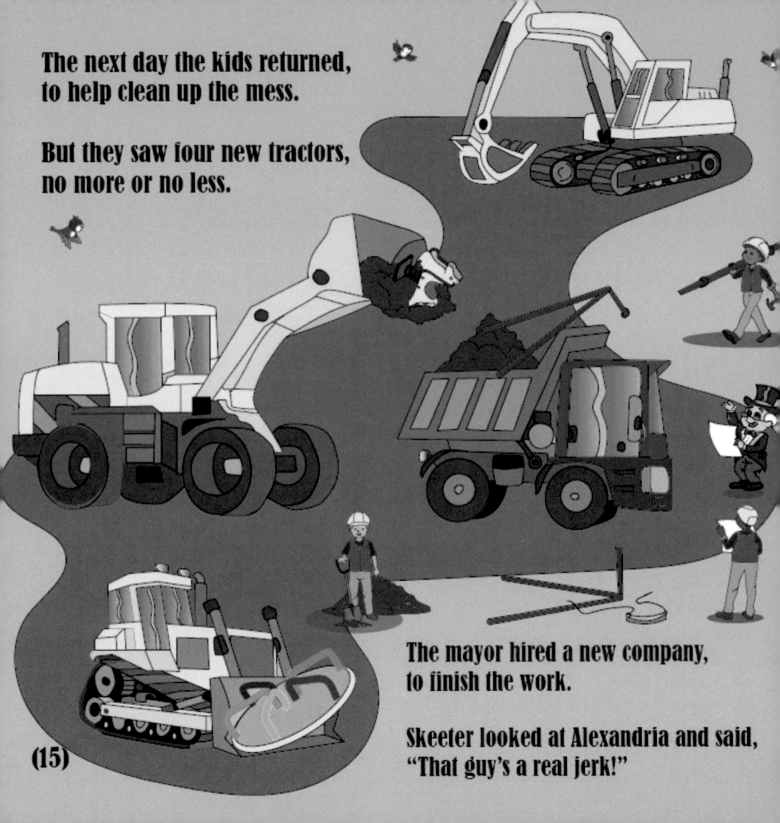

The next day the kids returned,
to help clean up the mess.

But they saw four new tractors,
no more or no less.

The mayor hired a new company,
to finish the work.

Skeeter looked at Alexandria and said,
"That guy's a real jerk!"

(15)

The mayor saw what happened,
and he was not pleased.

He pointed and screamed at the work crew,
"Knock down those trees!"

The men got on their machines,
and headed that way.

If the work went on,
the Enchanted Forest would be gone that da

(17)

The kids pleaded,
for the mayor to stop.

But he said, "If you don't leave,
I will call a cop!"

(18)

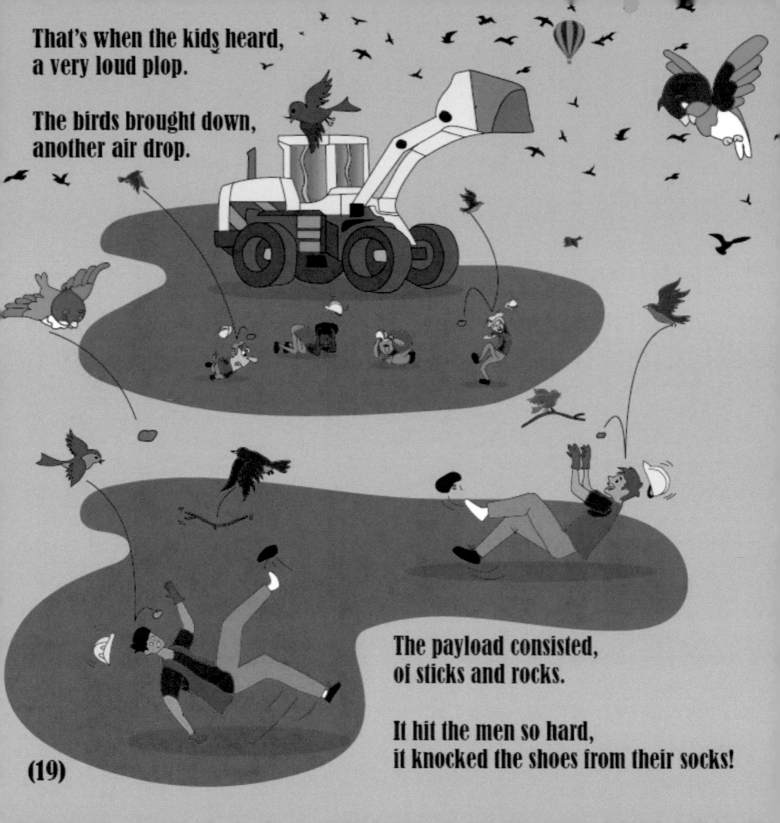

That's when the kids heard,
a very loud plop.

The birds brought down,
another air drop.

The payload consisted,
of sticks and rocks.

It hit the men so hard,
it knocked the shoes from their socks!

(19)

They brought all the machines,
to an almost crawl.
It was as if they had hit,
an imaginary wall.

Not only did the birds,
get in the way.
The rabbits and deers,
joined in on the fray.

All the animals worked together,
and heeded Alexandria's word.
They protected the Enchanted Forest,
like a magical herd.

(20)

The mayor was mad,
and he raised a fist with his hand.

"You all keep working,
we must clear off this land!"

(21)

The tractor's engines raced,
and the tires started to spin.

But all this commotion,
did not cause the animals to give in.

They stayed where they were,
and their courage did not waver.

Because down the road,
came a man with a favor.

(22)

It was Mr. Louse,
he had gotten his bulldozer running.

The kids asked him to help,
with their plan that was cunning.

They found Mr.Louse,
and pointed out one thing.

That when he was young,
he played on that very swing.

(23)

He destroyed the playground,
and felt bad for what he had done.

It weighed heavy on his heart,
almost a ton.

He knew deep inside,
that the kids were right.

He drove his dozer in the middle,
and pushed with all it's might.

(24)

He stopped all the tractors,
and they came to a halt.

If the forest was destroyed now,
It wouldn't be his fault.

Mr Louse yelled, "Don't you remember?
We all played here as a kid."

The other adults responded,
"We remember now. Yes we did."

(25)

Even the mayor's eyes,
began to flow tears.

Because he had forgotten the time,
he spent here all those years.

That's when the mayor declared,
"Now I understand!

The Enchanted Forest is precious,
We must preserve this land!"

The mayor felt bad and sobbed,
"I'm sorry I tore this whole place down.

But I vow I will fight,
to build an even better playground!" (26)

It was like a party,
the kids cheered and began to grin.

Everything worked out,
and even the animals jumped in.

Alexandria, Rusty and Skeeter,
started to gleam.

Because everyone, even the animals,
came together as a team.

(27)

The healing process had begun,
the trouble at the Enchanted Forest was done.

The mayor's promise came true,
the playground was rebuilt, for everyone, even you!

All animals need a place to live,
where they are not neglected.

Because every town has an Enchanted Forest,
that needs to be protected!

(28)

Please remember,
the world is a better place with you in it.
It doesn't matter if you're a boy or a girl- big or small, or
young or old.

You have a responsibility, to yourself,
to always do the next right thing.
You can make a difference.
The world is a better place with you in it.
Don't hesitate to help one another.
Choose love and always be kind.

I hope you enjoyed being part of the kids...
...good deed.

Keep the fun going and go make your own adventures!

THE END

DON'T MISS OUT ON THE KID'S OTHER ADVENTURES

FOLLOW ON:

FACEBOOK -- Frank Stangle
FACEBOOK GROUP-- Shiny Little Things-A Novel
INSTAGRAM--frankstangle
TWITTER--@FrankStangle
WEBSITE--www.frankstangle.com
EMAIL--frank@frankstangle.com

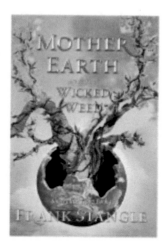

VISIT FOR MORE INFO

WWW.FRANKSTANGLE.COM

My gratitude goes out to everyone!

But a special thanks goes to:

Elliana "Ellie" Lazier, the smile you gave me when I read you the story before the pictures were done is priceless.   I will always remember it and it let me know that kids will love this story.

Alexandria Kayleigh,   you got so mad when you saw Mr. Louse wrecked the playground. I couldn't help, but laugh, and feel so bad at the same time. It was so cute!

Looking for more fun...

... go back into the story and find five hidden Snow Globes. I placed them in special loca-tions in the book. They may be hiding, so look closely.

This is what you are looking for.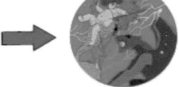

Made in the USA
Middletown, DE
23 June 2023

33290885R00022